What people are saying about "The Courage to Feel: A practical guide to the power and freedom of emotional honesty", now a best-seller.

"Andrew Seu
you to have
workable. It'
powerful." Bil

"...the book is a 'tour de force.' I don't know of anything in the literature that is such a comprehensive and clear guide to an understanding of the central role of emotions. It leads one to the 'courage to feel' and the rapture of being alive. Congratulations! You have done many a great service." *Clifford Smith, Ph.D.*

This is one of the seminal self-help books of the last 20 years!" *David Mandelbaum, Ph.D.*

"In the **Courage to Feel**, Andrew Seubert brings to bear the power and humility of true expertise in providing a guide to the process of "emotional honesty." *Michael P. Levine, Ph.D., FAED, co-author of* ***The Prevention of Eating Problems and Eating Disorders***

"I recommend this book to anyone who avoids telling themself the truth, or runs away from emotional honesty. Courage to Feel is a much needed resource for those who need to find another path." *Sandra Paulsen, author* ***Looking through the Eyes of Trauma and Dissociation***.

"I love this book! ***The Courage to Feel*** *is* my GPS of choice." *Mary Ellen Clausen, Executive Director, Ophelia's Place, Liverpool, NY*

"The Courage to Feel by Andrew Seubert is a book with *soul.* I read it; his words came alive with personal meaning for me. I was deeply touched by the heart-felt messages of his clients cited on these pages. Yes, it is a book with *heart*! " *B. Dick, Corning, NY*

"I'd read Daniel Goleman's *Emotional Intelligence* and was profoundly affected, but needed a more practical guide to take it to the next level. Your book was long overdue. " *J. Lovetti, New Mexico*

"I don't think I have ever before looked at all the emotions as a guidance system with hidden blessings, but the idea goes along totally with my belief in a loving Creator manifesting in a benignly evolving universe. ***The Courage to Feel*** could be a bridge between parent and child, a chance to respect feelings in a safe venue. For older children, like my fifth graders, it would legitimize their feelings." *J. Eidenier, elementary school teacher, PA*

"Unlike many self-help books, this one is not written in psych-speak, but in easy to digest, approachable language. Andrew's use of the turtle and the mouse is masterful. " *L.L., NY*

"Infrequently, a writer emerges who can capture complexity with exquisite simplicity, and such is the case with Andrew Seubert. His offering of ***The Courage To Feel*** reminds me of the wonderful work of John Lee, Bill O'Hanlon and John Bradshaw ." *D.C., PA*

"This book will leave you excited for your life. With humor, storytelling, and simplicity, Andrew guides us through the process of becoming more fully alive through emotional honesty. He shows us the possibilities that await and the barriers that can dissolve both within ourselves and our relationships when we practice these steps to being fully and authentically present in the moment. Andrew is a great teacher; he leaves us with clarity, enthusiasm and inspiration. I recommend this book to everyone who wants to live more joyfully." *S.C., DE*

"An empowering book! The ***Courage to Feel*** is a must read for anyone that wants to be authentic and real in all relationships, especially in relationship with themselves." *K.S., PA*

"***The Courage to Feel*** is my 'book of choice' to recommend to my UK clients. *J.Havens, UK.*

"I bought it for my son but found it so extremely well-written that I've been reading it each evening. I just purchased three more to begin lending to my clients, especially the avoidantly attached ones. You've done a wonderful job presenting a thorough description and explanation of all the ins and outs of an emotional life. I am highly impressed with how you've communicated this material and I know your book will meet the needs of many people. I'm confident many of my current and future clients will derive immense benefit. Thank you for putting emotional intelligence into such an enjoyable, compelling and accessible form." Charlette Mikulka, LCSW

"His own self-disclosures and those of the clients he writes about, exude a disarming, inviting quality. Instead of avoiding the truth the reader is gently coaxed into embracing it. I believe this is Andrew Seubert's greatest gift to the reader." *E.C., NY*

How Simon Left His Shell:
The Courage to Feel for Young People

By Andrew Seubert

Andrew Seubert

With a User's Guide

for Parent, Teachers and Therapists

ISBN 978-1-4958-0330-7 Hardcover
ISBN 978-1-4958-0636-0 Paperback
ISBN 978-1-4958-0637-7 eBook

Published March 2015

INFINITY PUBLISHING
1094 New DeHaven Street, Suite 100
West Conshohocken, PA 19428-2713
Toll-free (877) BUY BOOK
Local Phone (610) 941-9999
Fax (610) 941-9959
Info@buybooksontheweb.com
www.buybooksontheweb.com

Contents

Acknowledgements

Original concept for illustrations and original illustrations by Marc Rubin. Rendering of illustrations (based on the original concept) by Caitlin Turner. Each artist has signed their respective works.

******

A special thank you to David Mandelbaum, Ph.D. of Wilmington, DE and to Claire Malcolm, MSc of Calgary, Canada for their insights and feedback in the early stages of this work.

A Word at the Start...

In 2008, I published *The Courage to Feel: A practical guide to the power and freedom of emotional honesty.* I have come to learn that it has helped a great many people. It has even changed lives. I also realized that *The Courage to Feel* didn't speak to the younger people, particularly teenagers, who came into my office.

Youth is a tumultuous time of life, and it is made more so when the adults who surround them don't model emotional competency. Without mature emotional models, young people are left abandoned with their anger, their confusion, and their fears as they enter the journey of self-discovery. This realization planted the seeds that eventually gave birth to *How Simon Left His Shell: The courage to feel for young people.*

In my first book, the chapters are interspersed with a fable about a turtle named Simon. I used the fable in order to make the teaching in *The Courage to Feel* more vivid and interesting (self-help books, I must admit, can be boring beyond belief).

The fable centered on Simon's— journey of self-discovery to free the artist within him by leaving his shell. His hope was that then he would be free to paint scenes of his home in a southern marsh. Still, I felt that I was not reaching young people as directly as I wanted.

Consequently, I have expanded Simon's story to *How Simon Left His Shell* and added a "User's Guide for Parents, Teachers and Therapists." This experiential and interactive guide, with its questions and practice scenarios, uses the fable to teach young people to value and listen to their emotional guidance system and how to be emotionally competent in stormy times.

It is my hope that emotional competence and courage will prepare these future adults as they journey through relationships, marriages and families of their own into a world thirsty for healing waters that spring from the opened heart.

Andrew Seubert - 2014

How Simon Left His Shell:
The Courage to Feel for Young People

Chapter

The sun rises, peeks slowly over the hill and begins to warm tall grasses, still wet with the night's moisture. Light slips through the brush and falls upon something hard, something motionless.

Simon can feel the warmth of daybreak penetrate his home. He doesn't move for a while. Then, cautiously, he looks around his small world. Box turtles are like that.

Simon was incubated and hatched from an egg and quickly moved into his shell. Something inside told him that life was not always safe. Nothing was for sure! One could easily become turtle soup for someone if not careful. His mother, a nervous sort, modeled this to perfection. Protective, watchful, knowing there were dangers which could roll over her young turtle son in an instant, Turtle Mom taught Simon the ways of caution, preferring to be safe rather than sorry.

"Time for something to eat," Simon thinks. He begins his slow and deliberate routine of glancing around. He searches for insects, berries and juicy blades of grass. After he finds breakfast, he crawls back to his spot and pulls his head inside his shell. He notices the old contented feeling after a meal or, sometimes, that familiar nervous feeling in his turtle tummy: the feeling that always told him never to let down his shell. You just never know...

C. Turner

Chapter

For as long as Simon could remember, it was just he and his mother. Turtle Mom was a lovely lady, as turtles go, but she always had that scrunched-up look on her face. Simon could never tell if she was angry, had a headache, or a stomachache from eating the wrong kind of bug. He was too scared to ask! He just made sure he didn't upset her.

Simon didn't recall hatching from an egg or when he first moved into his shell. He only knew what his mother told him. He remembered being in his shell. Like forever! And, he made sure that he kept what his mother taught him in the front part of his turtle brain.

"Remember, Simon," she would say, "stay hidden, especially when I'm not around."

"Uh, sure, mom," he would reply, as his small, red eyes darted back and forth to make sure things were safe.

Early on, Turtle Mom would make her way slowly and carefully through the marsh grasses, creating a path for her baby son to follow. She stopped, occasionally, to nibble on a berry, an insect, or an unsuspecting worm. When he was younger, Simon preferred bugs. As he grew older, he preferred the berries and juicy grasses, just like his mom did.

Five or six summers had passed since his turtle memory began. He slept under a bed of dry leaves and grass for most of winter. He came out occasionally for a meal. After many of these long naps, the sun began to stay longer and feel warmer. The soil and leaves gave off a very different and pleasantly earthy aroma, signaling Simon that it was time to come out into the springtime marsh.

Simon wandered in search of food during the spring and summer months. He made small paths of his own. At times, he ventured into the edge of a slow stream or places where water collected in the wetland. He made sure never to go too far! He stayed close to what was safe and familiar.

Still, even though he could hear his mom's warnings, even though he could always picture that scrunched-up look on her face, he was curious, and also a bit... He didn't have a word for it, but he wondered and wondered: what else might there be beyond these narrow paths and the inside of his shell?

Chapter

It had been a while since Simon the Turtle poked his head a bit further out of his shell. Time had passed. He was noticing things now: things around him as well as things inside of him. It was a sunny afternoon as he dozed off, watching the red cardinals, yellow finches and all sorts of birds. It felt to him as if he were drifting up and into the blue sky and the white, cotton clouds... and he dreamed. He dreamt he was a lion living inside his shell, trying to roar, but he couldn't. His shell was too tight, too cramped. He awoke suddenly and felt a pushing and a longing, but he had no words for it. He only knew it would not go away.

The birds, colors, skies and clouds Simon was noticing wouldn't go away either. They became pictures, taking up residence inside his head. He began to think about the strangest thing. Strange, at least, for a turtle! He wanted those wonderful pictures inside him to last forever. He wanted everyone else to see them the way he did. He actually began to imagine himself...

"No, no," he thought. "That is just too weird for a turtle. After all, I have to live in my shell."

But those images wouldn't leave him. He dreamed again, but this time of leaving his shell behind, feeling nakedly free, and following the beautiful colors and critters of the world and... and, drawing and painting them! He awoke with the memory of a turtle without a shell, on a journey with no particular destination, carrying an enormous pencil over his shoulder.

"Oh, oh! Weird, bad, bad, weird! Turtle soup time!" Simon thought.

Yet the feelings pushing and straining inside his body wouldn't let up. He didn't really have names for them since turtles don't pay much attention to things outside, much less things inside. Simon knew he couldn't tell his mother about the dreams or what was happening inside him. She would tell him to ignore them and be content inside his shell where things were safe and sure. Yet the more time he spent noticing those pushings and yearnings, those fears and the excitement, the more he knew things would never be the same.

RUBIN

Chapter

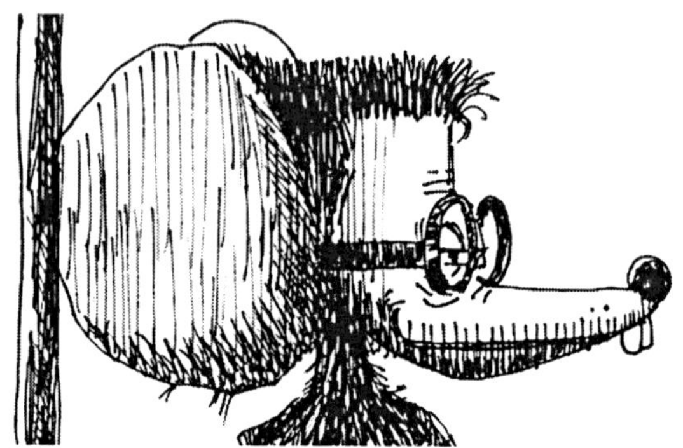

Simon was becoming a dysfunctional turtle. Usually calm, satisfied and agreeable, he found himself getting irritable, edgy. His shell began to feel more like a prison than a shelter, and Turtle Mom more like a prison guard. The corner of the marshland that had been his backyard no longer interested him. His dreams haunted him, and his feelings simply stockpiled, threatening to explode through his very shell.

Simon dreamed the dream of something bigger, something that felt, yes, felt as if a warm, brilliant sun was rising in his belly, then into his heart and head. He continued to see things, as if for the first time, and he so wanted to share his first sight with others. He saw himself in open spaces, learning from what others in the marshland had seen and been through, experiencing new things himself, and....and always drawing wonderful pictures of all the colors, plants and creatures who lived in the marsh, hanging his paintings from the low branches of willow trees so others could gaze upon what they had often noticed, but perhaps, now, could really see for the first time. "Isn't that what neighbors are for?" asked a voice inside his head that sounded just like the voice he had heard in his dreams.

So vivid and pressing were his dreams that, upon awakening, he was never quite sure if he was ending a dream and entering the real world, or if his dream was more real than his everyday life. He couldn't stay inside his shell, yet he was afraid to go. But, where? How?

On the inside of his shell, Simon began to feel different things. First, he was bored. Then scared. Then frustrated and more nervous. And the different feelings pounded back and forth inside. "How did they get in there?" he wondered. "Inside my shell!?!" He wasn't happy with his outside, even less happy with his inside world.

"Why can't I just be like other turtles and just be okay with what mom told me?" he would ask himself, often aloud. One day someone overheard him; someone who would soon provide the keys and answers to his questions and his dreams. It was a voice that was both tiny and strong. Sort of squeaky, but definitely with attitude.

"Because you're not and you can't!" came a small voice from just outside Simon's shell. Simon suddenly felt that pull in his stomach that said, "Beware! This could be soup time!" For once, however, he couldn't stand pulling further back into his shell just because something in his belly was crying, "Danger!"

"I mean, after all, it is a tiny voice, so it couldn't be any bigger than me... and I could always pull back into my shell. Right?"

"Right," agreed Tiny Voice.

"Oh-h-h-h, how did it know what I was thinking? Not good, not good."

"You're doing okay," said the voice. "You paid attention to your stomach, but then you used your turtle brain to see if your stomach was upset for a good reason or not. Head and heart. Nice job."

The voice was sounding less and less frightening. Simon slowly moved his pointed nose, eyes and then the rest of his head towards the opening of his shell. Peering outside, past the edge of his shell, he came nose to nose with... a T-shirt that said "Mighty Mouse".

"Who, uh, who are you?" asked Simon.

"Oh, just a mouse who's lived in this marsh a long, long time. I kind of know my way around. Thought I might be of some help."

Ronald was, to be truthful, a bit taken with himself; but, then again, mice who can read thoughts and who know things about brains and feelings are a bit hard to come by. Standing on his hind legs, front feet crossed in front of his chest, was a mouse whose entire body was no bigger than the opening of Simon's shell.

"Uh, uh, how did you know I needed help?" stammered Simon. Then, after a few moments, "I'm just so confused."

"I know," answered Ronald. "That's why I'm here."

Simon was at first relieved, then amused, and then, as moments passed, more and more curious. Here in a small corner of the marshland was the tiniest of creatures who for some unknown reason stirred the first bit of hope in a turtle heart that had been heavy for a long, long time.

• do you ever feel confused by your own emotions?
• do you ever ge frustrated by not fitting in with others?
• paid attention to your stomach, but then decided if it was a good reason or not.
• how could Ron. help Simon?
C. Turner

Chapter

Simon's head was out. It was no longer stuck inside his shell. He had poked his head out before, but just for a short while, and just to make his way around the small part of the swamp that had become his world. The tall cattails by the edge of the swamp, the one moss-covered log that lay flat in a few inches of dark water, and the familiar, dank odor had lost their sense of comfort for him.

Now, Simon wanted more, and he wanted to know what this mouse knew. How did this mouse become so, so… cocky, so sure of himself? He wanted to get more than his head out of his shell. He wanted to stretch his arms and legs. He wanted to wear a T-shirt, too.

Simon moved his head and neck beyond the edge of his shell into daylight. He heard that voice in his head once more. It was the voice that had been encouraging him to follow his dreams, his longing. It was the voice that had begun to teach him how to breathe when he felt nervous.

And so, with a huge breath, Simon began to push and pull his way out of his shell. Ronald watched and knew it wouldn't be easy.

"Come on, big guy!" encouraged Ronald. "You're almost out! Just keep on breathing! Breathe slow into your belly, then let it go!"

Simon did his best, but it wasn't enough. His shoulders were too tight, his chest puffed up. He was much too nervous.

"I, I can't do it! I just get more stuck!" cried Simon.

"Okay, okay. Slow down, big guy. Let me see..." and Ronald thought hard and fast. "Keep breathing the way I told you. Then think like, uh... I know! Think worm! Wiggle!! That's it! Think worm and then wiggle! Relax your shoulders, blow the air out of your chest, and very, very slowly wiggle out of your shell."

Simon did! He squirmed, pushed, stretched and wiggled!, All the while, he was aware of those feelings inside. Fear and excitement tumbled together in his belly and his chest. With his arms outside the shell, he grabbed the edges of his home, gave one last push! Plop! He found himself sprawled on the moist soil of the marsh!, He felt for the first time the glorious warmth of the sun on his back and shoulders. For the moment, all he noticed were the feelings of excitement and joy that grew and spread through his entire body. He had left home at last...

"What now, big guy?" asked Ronald.

And with that question, the fear resurfaced in Simon's stomach, and lunged its way into his chest.

“Oh, my,” answered Simon. “I hadn’t thought of that!”

Simon had not a clue. Not a single thought, but there was something inside his head. There were pictures of things he would draw and paint, pictures of himself carrying the perfect pencil over his shoulder, pictures of smiles on the faces of the mice, the snakes, the frogs, the birds who lived in the marsh and who would come to see Simon’s drawings.

Simon struggled to his feet, feeling somewhat naked, actually towering over the tiny, mighty mouse.

“I need a shirt,” he said to Ronald. “I feel too weird without my shell or anything else.”

Ronald pointed to a nearby willow tree, and hanging from the lowest branch, held up by two squirrels, was a T-shirt that said, “Big Guy”. Simon, now standing, tried out this walking thing. Earth and moss squeezed between his toes, as he swayed slightly from side to side. More feelings arose in his body, as he toddled over to the shirt, took it down from the squirrels, and clumsily pulled it over his head. Simon was officially out!

With his shell behind him, Simon now marveled at his new attire.

“How cool is this shirt?!” he exclaimed. “I never ever thought I could feel this, uh, this loose, this free!”

But a funny look slowly began to creep across his face.

“But what do I do now?” he asked Ronald.

“That’s up to you,” came the reply. “What makes your boat float?”

"I see pictures in my head. I want to draw them, paint them, so everyone really sees how cool this swamp really is. But I'm nervous. Real nervous."

"About what?" asked the mouse, looking up at Simon.

"About my mom. What she'll say if she catches me out of my shell?"

"Don't know," replied Simon. "But what's the worst thing she could say?"

"Well, she'd yell at me, scold me, tell me I'm bad or crazy or both for leaving my shell.".

"Is that the worst?" asked Ronald.

"Well, not really. Then she'd probably feel bad and start crying. I hate it when she does that. Just hate it!"

"So why do you hate it?" contir

"Well, I just start to feel really b

"Bad, like guilty?" Ronald ques

"Yeah, like I'm some slug, not

Ronald was thinking hard. His se turned up a bit, his eyes squinted.

"Listen, big guy, are you tryin

"No, not at all! Not at all!" Sir

"Is there any rule that says th ver and give up your dreams?" challenged Ronald further.

Simon gave this one some thought. He had never looked at all of this in

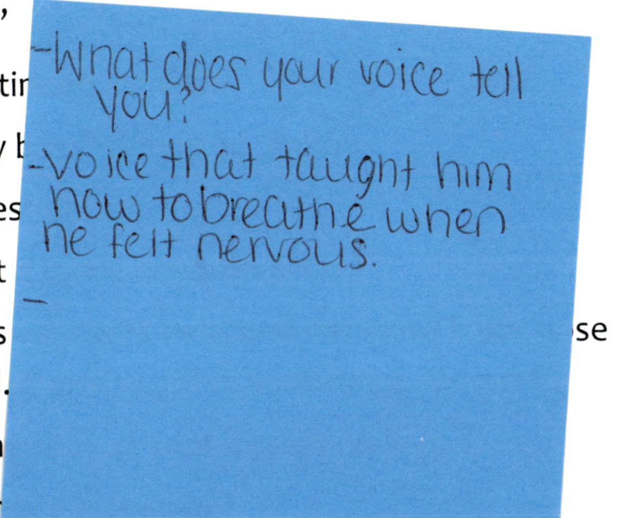

terms of unspoken rules.

"Guess not," Simon muttered.

"Then where do all these ideas of 'bad', or 'crazy', or both come from?" asked Ronald.

"Uh, from my mom, I guess."

At this point Ronald was poised at the height of logical brilliance. With an upward flip of his head, he folded his arms, drew himself up to his full mousy stature, and proclaimed, "Then you'll just have to leave them in your mom's head where they belong, not in your head....or else you'll never draw a line or paint a picture. Not ever!!"

C. Turner

Chapter

A light began to creep across Simon's face, a glint in his eyes. He and Ronald were facing each other in a small clearing, savoring the moment of revelation, when the cattails and grasses around them parted slowly. Simon heard rustling movement! He turned, horrified to see his mother, shell and all, entering the clearing with a look of shock and anger on her face.

"Simon! Simon Turtle!! What have you done!?! Cover yourself up right now!" Turtle Mom shrieked.

Simon froze. Ronald deflated a bit. There they were, Mighty Mouse and Big Guy, caught by the Ultimate Enforcer.

"Uh, uh…well, uh…" Simon stuttered.

"Speak up!" his mom demanded, now a mix of fury and fear covering her face. "What has happened to you? What will the other turtles think?"

Simon's brain had gone offline. He couldn't think, speak or even see straight. Everything around him blurred. All he could see was his mother's face and that look of shock and anger -- the LOOK that could penetrate the biggest rock or the widest tree trunk.

Then he felt a nudge from behind. In his panic, he had forgotten that Ronald was still there, gathering up his own wits.

"Breathe! Remember? Breathe!" Ronald whispered.

Simon listened once again to the small voice, began to breathe. His vision began to widen just a bit.

"Relax your shoulders!"

Simon wasn't even aware that his shoulders were touching his ears. He was as tense as a board all over! He followed the instructions and began to notice his brain clearing up and words beginning to form in his head.

"Uh, uh, Mom, I just gotta do this. Otherwise, I'll... I'll never be happy."

Now it was mostly fear that sat heavily on his mother's face.

"But Simon, it's so dangerous out there... and you're ignoring all that I've taught you... "

Simon could feel heat creep across his face. It felt as if he was ruining everything for everyone.

"Go, big guy! One thought at a time," whispered Ronald.

Simon breathed slowly again.

"Mom, I know, I know it can be difficult living outside the shell and outside our part of the swamp," Simon managed, " I'm just not happy there anymore. I'm scared! I'm excited, too, for the first time in my life. And I am making new friends!"

"You mean that rodent?!" his mother snapped.

Ronald winced, but knew enough to stay out of the conversation.

"Mom, his name is Ronald, and he's become a great friend. He helped me come out of my shell! And now he's helping me do the one thing I've always dreamed of. You know, painting all those pictures. I could never stop those dreams, Mom, because they were telling me what would make me happy. And Ronald is showing me how to take care of myself in the open swamp, just like you've taught me to take care of myself in our part of the swamp. Look, he gave me this yellow "Big Guy"shirt to keep me covered!"

"Smooth move!" Ronald noted to himself.

"I just have to make pictures for others to see. What do you say, Mom? I'll make the first one for you!"

"Oh, this guy is good!" Ronald thought.

Simon's mother was softening. She was clearly nervous, very nervous, but beginning to realize she could not control her son's life.

"If I might add something, ma'am?" ventured Ronald.

"Squeak up, I can't hear you!" added Simon's mom, a bit sarcastically. After all, she had to blame someone for being upset.

Covering up his annoyance, Ronald said, "I'd be nervous, too, if he was my son. It's like a bird in a nest. If momma bird keeps the baby safe in the nest, the young one never learns to fly."

Simon's mother was impressed. This mouse had more behind his whiskers than his nose.

"Hm-m-m-m," she murmured, as her own feelings quieted down and her brain began to clear. "You might have a point. But Simon might get hurt!"

Yes, ma'am," replied Ronald, "but with his new friends and you to check on him each day (he looked over at Simon who flinched a tad), he might get hurt from time to time! We'll help him up; he will get stronger. And then, he'll paint his swamp world in pictures. And I'm not sure why, but it's like this is what your son is meant to do. Know what I mean? To make this a better swamp. I think his happiness radar is speaking to him.

"And when he gets to do all this, it will be so amazing….and it will be your son doing all that!"

They grew quiet in the clearing. Visions of possibilities arose among them silently. The sun began to retreat, as the swamp slipped into evening silence. Yet they all knew the light would return.

The world was becoming bigger. Their hearts were beating a bit faster as they felt the fears and excitement. They also felt something unusual, something none of them had a word for. They felt it in their throats and just behind their eyes. It had something to do with being in that clearing together and leaving old ways behind. It had to do with the sun warming them, marshy paths inviting them. It had to do with being together and part of something larger than they had ever imagined.

C. Turner

Chapter VII

Not much time had passed since Simon announced his new way of life to his mother. He found favorite spots in the swamp where he would set up his easel and paintbrushes. Once in a while, he passed his old chomping grounds and his abandoned shell. Often, he would spy Turtle Mom lying there, her head hanging out of her shell, with that same look.

"I just hate that look!" he told Ronald one cloudy morning.

"What look?" asked the mouse.

"The angry one! Like she's not going to forgive me, no matter what, for leaving my shell."

"And...?" prodded Ronald.

"And then I feel sort of bad," Simon replied.

"Where in your turtle body?"

"Uh, my stomach, and a little bit in my face," said Simon.

"And what's this 'bad'?"

"Well, you know, guilty. I push it away for a while, but it always comes back, and then I feel worse."

"Okay, okay, review lesson number one," stated Ronald. "Did you do something wrong to your mother? Break any agreement?"

"No," replied Simon.

"All right, then we have a false alarm. And what set the alarm off?" persisted Ronald.

"I told you, it's the look!" answered Simon impatiently.

"A look is a look until you put a story to it. What's your story?" asked Ronald.

"That she's mad because I left," came the reply.

"And where does the story come from?" asked Ronald, drawing himself up once again, as he closed in for the big question.

"From her?" quizzed Simon.

"You don't know that, do you?"

"From ME?" Simon asked in amazement.

"Maybe. Only one way to find out, isn't there?"

After the full impact of Ronald's questioning sank in, Simon made his way through the reeds, around weathered logs, to the place where his mother would be resting. He found her taking in the sun in a small clearing near the water's edge. She lifted her head, somewhat surprised, still with that look.

"Mom," Simon stammered, " I... I need to talk to you about something."

"About what?" she replied. "You've made your decision."

With that statement, his guilt resurrected.

"Well, you look so angry, Mom. Are you?"

"I was, but not anymore," she stated cautiously.

"But that look, that look on your face...!" he said.

"Oh, Simon, I've always had that look. Even as a baby turtle, my mother said I frowned all the time. Like I had swallowed a spider or something."

"So you're not angry?" Simon asked, holding his breath.

"No, no. I think I'm over that. But I think I get that look when anything bothers me. And right now, I guess I'm just afraid. Afraid that you'll get hurt..." she murmured.

"Oooh," muttered Simon with relief, as his story and his guilt faded. "Well, then maybe we could, uh, find some berries and have lunch together."

"That would be so nice," replied his mother. "Very nice."

C. Turner

Chapter VIII

Ronald peered over Simon's shoulder one morning as the turtle painted on his canvas! What Ronald saw on the painting resembled nothing he had ever seen in the swamp. Thick layers of red and black paint swirled into each other.

"Bad hair day?" quipped the mouse.

"Not funny, not funny at all," Simon grumbled angrily.

"Sorry, big guy. No offense. What's going on? I've never seen anything like that before."

"Oh, I'm just grumpy, irritated, frustrated. Not sure why, but that's what it feels like," Simon responded said, pointing to the canvas.

Ronald thought for a moment, and then ventured, "Is this more mom stuff?"

"Yeah, I think so. When I think of her being scared and all, I just get angry. Don't know why. I mean, she's not doing anything wrong. Nothing like that."

"Why don't we just hang out with that red and black stuff and see what happens?" suggested Ronald. "It's like asking if there's anything else there, maybe underneath the reds and blacks. Then you just wait for the answer."

"Not sure what you mean by waiting for the answer," questioned Simon.

"It's like sitting by the pond, tossing a stone into the middle of it, then waiting to see what kind of ripples come up," responded Simon.

"Oh, yeah, I think I can do that!"

And so, a bit of time passed, as Simon sat in front of his painting, and images of his frightened mother with "that look" passed through his head.

"Hm-m-m," muttered Simon. "It's not as strong now."

"You mean the irritation?"

"Yeah. It's not as strong. Funny, but it just sort of feels sad. Almost like there's a sad color underneath the black and that irritation. I think I need a different color."

C. Turner

Chapter

There were days when some of Simon's sadness about his mother still lingered, when his paintings didn't look that good to him, when he simply didn't know where his life was going. These were the hardest days of all.

All kinds of emotions would come crashing over him. In one moment, he was sad, then angry, then afraid, then bored, then nervous, then frustrated. They were so many that he couldn't make sense of all the signals coming at him so quickly. He wondered if his feeling radar was on the blink.

"What's going on with me?" he asked Ronald, who had stopped by on his way to one of the far ends of the swamp.. "All these feelings, and I just get more and more confused, then just sort of nothing!."

"Sometimes we just don't know. We can't go back to the way things were, and we don't know how or where to go forward. It's a hard place to be in. Like in the middle of nowhere."

"So, what do I do? I mean, have you ever had that problem? You always seem to know where you're going."

"Well, it wasn't always that way for me" replied Ronald.

"What do you mean, Ronald?" asked Simon.

"Oh, that's a story for another time. The main thing that I learned was that you have to wait it out and trust that there's something better on the other side of feeling stuck or empty."

"Even though I don't have a clue about what's on that other side? That fox could be there! Scary! Nothing could be there!"

"Yep, that does make it scary," replied Ronald. "I used to think that I always had to know what to do, that I always had to do something. Not knowing what was next and not doing anything together felt like too much, so I just got busy. But that usually didn't work.

"I remember, in that city up north where I got started, feeling real antsy and frustrated all the time. Then I'd get so bored. What I did then was to get busy, helping all kinds of mice out, especially the old ones, making a whole bunch of new mouse holes. Busy, busy, busy.

"But nothing changed until I stopped and just hung out with my irritation and boredom. At some point, all those feelings passed, and,well, it was kind of funny, totally new for me, but the quieter I got, the more I heard this voice in my head."

"You heard voices?" asked Simon.

"Actually, it wasn't like a real voice, more like a loud thought. But somehow I knew what the problem was. It just came to me. I knew I had to get out of that city."

"Is that how you got here?" Simon inquired with great interest.

"It was the first step," replied Ronald. "Then all sorts of things happened, and eventually I met you!"

"But what kind of things happened before we met? asked Simon, more curious than ever.

"Oh, not enough time for all of that. But after I took care of my friends in the alley where we lived – y'know, they used to call me the Prince of the Alley! – and after I made sure they knew how to look out for that cat that was always looking for a meal, I took off early one morning."

"And then?" asked Simon.

"Well, I had to duck under car wheels and run from screaming humans, but I finally found my way to a railroad yard. Y'know, with all those trains waiting to leave. And I heard that voice again. "Do it!" it said.

"Do what?" queried Simon.

"Hop on the train. So I did! I listened to the voice, curled up in that baggage car, and when I woke up from a nap, the train had stopped not too far from our swamp."

"Amazing," said Simon. "Just amazing! So that train kind of brought us together."

"Sure did," replied Ronald. "And it was because I just listened."

"So, what do I do now?" wondered Simon out loud.

"Not much," was the mouse's reply. "Just be still, let things pass, and listen for that voice. Yep, listen for that voice!"

B
C. Turner

Chapter

Simon just didn’t get it! When he lived in his shell, things were predictable. Critters were simply critters. He did what his mother advised. There was a time and a place for everything.

Now, on his own, Simon’s world was so much more confusing. Not only were there days when the swamp held one surprise after another, but creatures and things didn’t stay the same. The bullfrog was one such animal.

On some evenings, the deep voices of the bullfrogs seemed like music, resonant and rhythmic… Ribbitt! Ribbitt! Ribbitt!. At other times, those same voices were unbelievably irritating… Ribbibbitt Ribbibbitt! At those times, Simon wished he could pull his old shell back over his head!

Evening could be soothing at times, frightening at others. The sun was warm and inviting in one moment, but without his shell, Simon often felt the heat of the day burning his body! The same creatures, the same events were really never the same.

Most interesting were his reactions to those closest to him: his mother and his dear friend, Ronald. Oh, how he appreciated his mom sometimes! She always did her best to be there for him. At other times, however, she seemed more like the wicked witch of the swamp, a jail keeper! It was somewhat the same with Ronald. He could be the best friend a turtle could have. He could also seem to be just an irritating mouse with attitude.

"Appearances change," Simon thought. "Why is that? Why don't things stay the same?"

"Because you don't stay the same," came the edgy voice of the mind-reading mouse. Whenever Simon ran into these dilemmas, Ronald had the sometimes annoying habit of popping up almost out of nowhere, inevitably with the right answer.

"Now that makes no sense," replied Simon with some irritation. "Things are supposed to be the way they are!"

"And who says so?" asked Ronald. "Think of it this way. If you had a tummy ache, like the time you ate that weird bug and your stomach felt kind of sour and upside down, how did things look to you for most of that day

"Awful," recalled Simon. "If I had to color that day, I would color it green and grey."

"Exactly!" replied Ronald, puffing up. "And if you have a headache, is your mom more annoying? If you're feeling confused and irritated, do I get on your nerves?"

"Yep, on both counts," answered Simon.

"So, with both things and people, we don't really see them as they are, do we? We see them as we are. Do you get it now??"

"Oh, oh, my," stammered Simon, as a light seemed to go on somewhere in the middle of his turtle brain.

C. Turner

Chapter

Weeks passed! Ronald noticed that Simon was growing a bit distant from everyone. He stayed by himself a lot, his shoulders slumped and his head drooping. He was back in his moping mode. He was still painting the swamp critters, but he didn't seem to connect with them as much. The bullfrogs, the beavers, and the masked raccoon wondered if they had done something to offend Simon, since he was so silent. Even the fox, who didn't have much to do with anyone, noticed the change. The fox lay at the edge of the woods and quietly watched.

Ronald sighed and pulled himself up, realizing it was time to do something about it. He made his way through the grass and the reeds at the water's edge, until he was standing next to Simon.

"What's up, big guy?" he began.

"Nothing. Nothing at all!"

"I don't believe you," said Ronald flatly. "You're moping again."

"So?" Irritated, Simon put down his brushes and shuffled over to the edge of a log.

"So, something's going on, and you're not talking. You don't look all that happy. As a matter of fact, you look ticked off!"

"Well, maybe I am," sputtered Simon. "Maybe I'm tired of those beavers slapping their tails in the water all the time. Maybe I'm annoyed at that bullfrog's weird voice. Maybe I don't know if raccoon plans to steal one of my brushes or not. And I hate the way that fox stares all the time.

"You know, they don't realize how hard it is to concentrate out here. It's like I'm invisible, or that what I'm doing isn't important to them. Can't they see what I'm doing, what I'm painting? Don't they get it?"

"Probably not," said Ronald. "How are they supposed to know?"

BG
C. Turner

Chapter

Simon and Ronald sat on a favorite log by the water. A perfect day in the swamp! Flies and bees hummed peacefully, willow leaves rustled slightly, and water trickled past on its journey through the swamp. Simon had his best friend right next to him.

"You know," began Simon, "everything seems so right today. I like how I feel right now. Especially, I like how I feel with you right beside me."

Ronald nodded, but remained quiet for a few moments.

"What're you thinking?" asked Simon, noticing his friend's unusual reticence.

"Remember we were talking the other day, and you said that sometimes I can irritate you?" answered Ronald.

"Yeah, I remember," replied Simon. "But that doesn't happen too often, you know."

"Right, but do you like how you feel at times like that? I don't mean irritated or angry or such things. I mean, how you are feeling about Simon when I'm irritating you."

"Ummm, not so good," answered Simon.

"Well, that could be a problem."

"How so?" asked Simon.

"You know how your mom's look can upset you?"

"Uh, huh! For sure!" was Simon's quick reply,

"As we say up North, when momma ain't happy, ain't nobody happy."

"So what are you trying to tell me?" asked Simon. Ronald simply continued.

"And if beaver, bullfrog, raccoon and fox all irritate you, and you can't be okay, you can't feel good about Simon when they're just living their lives – remember, making sounds, staring at you, those kinds of things? And you don't say anything to anybody... Well, that's the problem. I mean, if we're okay only if someone else is okay, or only if they're acting the way we want them to act... it's like being a yoyo at the end of someone else's string."

"Uh, what's a yoyo?"

"Oh, just some kind of toy. Yeah, like being someone else's toy. Hey, big guy, this is kind of deep, you know. If I'm okay only if you're okay, or if you're okay only if I'm okay and not annoying you, then we don't have a friendship. We have a prison where nobody is ever free. We just can't be ourselves."

"Confusing," said Simon. "Very, very confusing!"

He paused thoughtfully, and then quietly went on. “But I wonder if it’s like feeling down whenever it’s cloudy and okay only when the sun shines. You know what I mean? I’m okay if the sky is okay…”

“Impressive, big guy,” said Ronald, a large grin spreading under his whiskers. “Impressive, indeed.”

Chapter XIII

"You still look confused," commented Ronald later that day. He and Simon moved through tall, summer grass. The sun was setting behind the edge of the marsh, accompanied by a chorus of bullfrogs, tree frogs, and crickets. "Still wondering about that irritated thing?"

"Nope," replied Simon, "this is a different confusion. I'm not sure what it's about, but evenings are the worst. Especially when we're near my old shell."

Simon nodded his head to the left where his empty turtle shell lay, overgrown with brush and moss.

"I get really sad, but then sort of relieved and even a bit excited. Then the sadness again. More confusion!" Simon muttered.

Ronald always had an answer. Socrates of the swamp. "Do you remember what it was like the first few times I had to be away? How sad you were? And how glad you were that we had become such good friends?"

"Yeah, like sad and glad at the same time," chirped Simon.

"Right," said Ronald. "Sometimes it works like that."

"But what does that have to do with my shell... and the evening?" asked Simon.

"What's it like when you think of your shell and of your life in the shell?"

"Well, that's confusing, too," answered Simon. "Like something was ending and something else was beginning. The ending was scary, but sad, too, because I was there for so long. It was like losing an old friend."

"Any other reason why it might be sad to think of all those years in the shell?" pursued Ronald.

"Oh, yeah, all that time not painting. Just listening to what my mother told me to do. And, and there's something else missing, something else that's sad, but I can't put my toe on it."

Ronald continued. "And when you think of finally leaving the shell, what does your radar tell you then?"

"It feels like I escaped, it's exciting!"

"There you have it," concluded Ronald, "all at once. Amazing isn't it?"

"But what about the evening part?" asked Simon.

"Well, what happens to the day when evening comes?" asked Ronald, unflappable as usual.

""Oh-h-h," came the reply. "It's OVER!."

"Exactly. And sometimes 'over' is sad and glad at the same time. Isn't it?"

"Now I get it, YES, I get it!" Simon exclaimed, as they continued their evening stroll past the old, abandoned shell.

C. Turner

Chapter

It was a day when the world seemed to be wearing a heavy, grey coat. The marsh seemed out of breath, as clouds settled in over the reeds and water. Ronald leaned against their favorite log, staring off somewhere into the willow trees. Simon, on his way to the pond, was a bit surprised to see his friend in the middle of the day, just sitting and gazing. Not doing anything.

"Uh, what's up, Ronald?" asked Simon.

"Oh, grey days get to me sometimes."

"How do you mean?" replied Simon.

"Days like this get me thinking. I was remembering that cat, where I used to live. And what was going on for me then. I can still see that city up North. Cold and dirty. Felt like living in a garbage pail! And I remember that cat in the alley. Kind of fat, mostly grey with white paws and big, big claws. And that evil and orange look in his eyes. We called him Dodo! I always wondered what went on inside his furry head.

"Is this that story you said was for another time?"

"Guess so. I still feel sad about the old man..."

"What old man?" Simon was curious.

"Oh, I think I told you about him." responded Ronald, as if half in a dream.

"You mean the one you helped out?"

"Yeah, yeah. Him. He's the one."

Ronald's eyes moistened. It scared Simon. He had never seen his friend like this before. A few round tears made their way to the edge of his whiskers

"You okay?"

"Sure. Just gimme a minute."

"Well, it scares me to see you like that!" Simon ventured cautiously.

"Nothing to be scared about, big guy. Just gotta let it loose. I really miss my old friend. Did I ever tell you how we met?"

"No," answered Simon.

"Well, I never really knew who my parents were. When I was old enough to notice things, I realized that I didn't have a family like the other mice. Maybe the cat got them. I don't know. But one day the old guy, who wasn't so old then, pulled me aside and started to teach me some things."

"Like you do for me?"

"Yeah, sort of like that. He told me that I was okay, even without parents..."

Ronald's voice got caught somewhere in his throat. A few more tears slipped down his nose and onto his whiskers. He breathed, and then went on. Simon continued to be nervous. What if something inside of Ronald broke?

"He taught me about the cat," his voice a bit shaky, " how to get to food before the others, how to make it in the alley. He would always say, 'Go for it, Ronald. Go for it!' We had great talks, especially on those evenings when the moon was full and threw some light on the alley. Funny, that alley was like my shell, but I could never leave it while he was still there. He was my home."

"And you had to stay there as long as he was around?"

"Right. At least that's how I felt. He was like the only parent I ever had. Then as I got older, he got very old. So old, he needed someone to watch out for him. Until he died…"

Ronald got quiet. Very quiet, as his little shoulders shook.

For Simon, it was as if his world were coming apart, seeing his dear friend and teacher so very sad.

"Ronald! What can I do? It's okay, it's okay! I...I hate to see you like this!"

Simon's stomach and chest shook and then tightened.

"Just sit by me, that's all. That's what I need. Nothing you can do."

Simon remembered to breathe. Minutes passed that for Simon seemed to stretch forever.

"These waves just come and go sometimes. Just have to ride them."

"Do they ever stop?" asked Simon. Ronald paused to catch his breath.

"Well, I don't know if they'll ever completely stop," replied Ronald, as he finally took a deep breath. "I'll always miss him. And certain things will always remind me of him. Like when I'm able to find food for a meal, or when the moon comes up over the hills. Or when I wash my "Mighty Mouse" t-shirt. You know, it was his last present to me before his sight started to go."

Now it was Simon whose eyes were getting blurry.

"And when I get the chance to teach you things, I think of him, too."

Simon's tears began to fall. Ronald glanced over at him, waiting.

"I never knew my dad either," Simon muttered.

Moments passed. Everything felt heavy, as if the clouds were trying to squeeze more air out of the marsh.

"How come your story's so, so warm and fuzzy, sort of, and so sad at the same time?" asked Simon.

Ronald looked over at his friend. He seemed to know the answer, but was trying to find his little voice. He breathed again.

"Well, maybe because what feels so good is something we miss... or maybe something we never had."

Ronald sighed and turned towards a clump of bright yellow wildflowers. He plucked a few petals, and handed one to Simon.

"What's this for?" asked Simon.

"Blow your nose...!"

C. Turner

Chapter

Like clouds and seasons and rivers that run on and on, Ronald's heavy feelings passed. One morning soon after, a strange sight greeted him. He was passing the place where Simon had left his turtle shell. Ronald was used to glancing at it to see how overgrown it had become. He always grinned at the thought of how far Simon had come since their first meeting. Today, when he looked at it, however, he saw a sight he was not likely to forget.

Simon was beside his old shell! It looked as if he was trying to get back in. His head was buried inside the shell, the rest of his body sticking out, butt to the wind.

"Simon, buddy," exclaimed Ronald, "what's going on!? You trying to get back into that shell?"

"No!" came Simon's muffled voice from inside the shell. "I'm just hiding."

Ronald chuckled. "Well, it's not your best side that I'm seeing, big guy, and it's hard to miss."

"This is NOT funny. Not funny at all!"

"Okay, so what's going on?" repeated Ronald.

"I did something terrible last evening. Really bad!" said Simon.

"What did you do that was so bad?"

"You know how I get frustrated with the bullfrogs," said Simon, as he slowly extracted his head from the shell, "and their noisy voices when I'm trying to paint?"

"Yeah."

"Well, last evening I couldn't take it any more. I threw my paints – the yellows, the greens, blacks, blues – all of them! And then my brushes! All of it, I threw all of it into their pond! Then I watched the water turning these awful colors, and the smell took over everything in the pond. Then I screamed at them, over and over. They finally shut up, but ..."

"But what?" asked Ronald.

"I could see their faces," Simon went on. "Even the baby frogs. They all looked scared. And they couldn't get into the water with the paint in it. I feel just awful. So I'm hiding my face so no one can see me."

"Yep, not good," replied Ronald. "But what's hiding your head going to do?"

"I just don't want anyone to see me," said Simon. "They must think I'm the worst turtle in the swamp."

"Maybe, but that doesn't make it so."

"But I AM horrible!" said Simon.

"Well, doing bad and being bad aren't the same thing," replied Ronald impatiently, "in case I've never put it to you that way."

"But I feel so bad!" exclaimed Simon.

"But remember, how you feel is not who you are. You're always an okay turtle, even when you blow it!"

"Then how do I get this feeling to quit? It's killing me!"

"Well, first of all," replied Ronald, "you've got to stop building up and then blowing up. If you speak up sooner, then the other critters might understand you better, and you just might learn something about them."

"Anything else I need to know?" asked Simon, smarting a bit from the reprimand, gentle as it was.

"Well, those tough feelings might let up if you stop beating up on yourself! Get your head out of the shell, and do something different to make it up to the frogs," said Ronald firmly. "Hiding your head won't get you anywhere, and it won't fix the pond."

C. Turner

Chapter XVI

"But I never did anything like that before," moaned Simon, "I never threw paints and brushes into a frog pond, into someone else's home!. I just can't go back there!!" Simon imagined the terror of going back to the pond and facing the frog families. The thought brought a flush of red to his face and left him shaken!

"No choice?" said Ronald, bluntly. "Yes! you do have a choice. Don't do anything different. Just stick your head in the shell again. Just live with that guilt and feeling like you're the worst turtle this pond has ever seen. Or, you can let your guilt teach you something."

"Like what?" lamented Simon.

"Like making amends. Your temper took over and you hurt some folks. Tell them how crummy you feel! Tell them that you'll figure out how to clean up the mess you made. And then, see what happens to that guilt."

"But, I'm really, really scared!"

"Of what?" asked Ronald. "What's the worst thing that could happen?

They make fun of you? They stay angry with you? They croak louder at night?"

"Yeah, all of that," replied Simon.

"Even if that did happen, how would you be feeling, knowing that you did the right thing? Or would you rather live with that guilt forever?"

"No, nothing's worse than that!," a wide-eyed Simon quickly responded.

"So," came Ronald's finale, "if nothing changes, then nothing changes!"

C. Turner

Chapter XVII

"You know," Simon told Ronald as they watched the lily pads float on the clear pond water, "I finally had that conversation with the frogs." He paused. "They thought that all turtles were temperamental and disrespectful."

"No surprise," replied Ronald. "No surprise at all."

Simon had kept his word, cleaning up the mess he had made of the pond water with a bunch of cattails. Then he had a heart-to-heart talk with several of the frog elders.

"But why no surprise?" asked Simon. "After all, I'm just one turtle, not all turtles. And I'm not even a very average turtle."

"Did they feel the same way after you had that talk with the elders?" asked Ronald.

"No, I guess talking changed it all. Before that, they didn't know me at all."

"Did you know much about them, other than their singing every evening?"

“That wasn’t singing!” snapped Simon, but quickly caught himself.

“Maybe it wasn’t singing to you, but to them, it’s kind of what keeps them connected, like a family,” said Ronald.

“Oh,” replied Simon. “I didn’t know…”

C. Turner

Chapter XVIII

Ronald was talking about what Simon and the bullfrogs were learning from each other.

"So, they thought you were temperamental and disrespectful, right?"

"Yep, they were totally convinced," Simon answered.

"And you had no clue how important their evening croaking was to them, did you?"

"Nope."

"If that situation had continued, can you imagine what might have happened?"

"That's a very bad picture," replied Simon, after a few moments. "They probably would have made as much noise as possible, especially when I needed quiet. And I can see myself throwing more paint at them."

"And what do you think would happen if word of this spread around the swamp?"

“I’m afraid that a lot of frogs and turtles would start to take sides. They’d start to dislike each other even if they’d never met.”

“Most likely,” said Ronald. “More croaking, more shouting, more oil paint in the water all through the swamp.”

“Like war,” said Simon.

“Exactly.”

C. Turner

Chapter

Chapter XIX

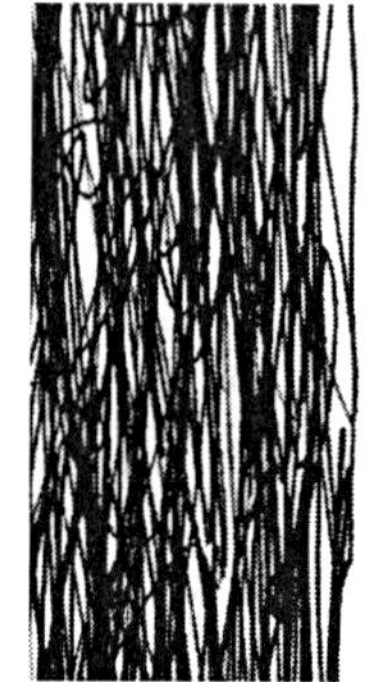

The afternoon was warm and muggy. Without his shell, Simon had to seek out the shade of a large willow tree. Ronald tagged along as usual, still not ready to leave his new friend on his own. After all, a turtle without a shell in a huge wetland felt to him like a disaster looking for an opportunity. And he had promised Simon's mother that he would look after her son.

Simon sat and leaned against the trunk of the tree. His head began to droop almost immediately. Ronald was quick to notice.

"What's the matter, pal? You've been moping again."

"Dunno," answered Simon. "Something's just not right."

"Miss your shell?" asked the mouse.

"No, no, nothing like that," said Simon. "I just don't know. Just don't feel that excitement anymore."

It had been a month or so since Simon had left his shell and the tiny part of the marshland that he called home. He had left with his drawing pencils. He and Ronald were searching for beautiful things and scenes in the wetlands to draw. He had drawn a majestic willow tree, a butterfly, and an orange wildflower that hung like a lantern. That was all in the first day. Since then he hadn't drawn a thing.

"And I had a dream last night," said Simon. "Kind of scared me."

"About what?" asked Ronald.

"Well, I dreamed that my pencils were too big to pick up. Then my drawing pad was sort of greasy, and I couldn't draw on it. Then a huge wind came along, picked me up, and dropped me in a strange part of the swamp. No pencils, no pad, no shell. And when I woke up, my chest was tight, and I was breathing real heavy. And the fox was staring at me!"

"Ah, another day in Happy Land!" quipped Ronald.

"It's not funny, really," said Simon.

"Sorry, sorry," answered Ronald. "But you seem so, so bleak and hopeless. Do you ever get afraid that you made a mistake in leaving the shell?"

"Everyday," said Simon. "Like I'm afraid to go on, but if I don't, I'll never know. And then I'd probably be sad forever from not having tried."

"Tried what? Drawing? Leaving home?"

"They're the same thing to me," said Simon. "But I'm so scared that I won't make it as a swamp artist. And no home and all that dream stuff... "

Ronald folded his arms across his small body, a sign that he was about to hold forth.

"Suggestion?" he asked Simon.

"What?"

"Draw two things. Draw a picture of yourself when you're afraid and one of yourself drawing yourself when you're afraid. See which one feels better…"

Hours slipped by as Simon lost himself in Ronald's suggestion. The two images slowly emerged. In one, he was his fear. In the other, he was watching it.

Simon hung the two drawings from the lowest limb of the willow tree. When he focused on the picture of himself being afraid, he felt a twinge in his stomach. Then he became angry and sad, almost simultaneously. The scared face looked like he had felt all those years in the shell. He felt his chest and throat tightening and found it hard to breathe.

Then he stared at the picture of himself drawing that first picture. Something lifted. Energy began to move throughout his entire body. The excitement was returning! The image of himself drawing the scared face, and not just being it, set something free inside of him. Instead of tumbling down a river of fear, he could sit on the bank, question it, and watch it flow by.

Finally, he was ready to do what he had set out to do when he first left his shell. Ready to face fear, give it a name, learn what he could from it, and still listen to that voice.

He smiled gratefully at Ronald and headed down the path to the edge of the pond, where his easel and a chorus of bullfrogs awaited him.

C. Turner

Chapter XX

At times, Simon painted from the inside out. The shapes and colors on his canvas flowed from whatever he was feeling at the moment. They didn't resemble anything that lived in the swamp, but seemed to choose themselves. He did this best with his eyes closed.

Ronald passed by the painting pond, as they now called it! On this morning, Simon sat with his eyes closed in front of his easel. He didn't move and wasn't touching his brushes. Ronald watched for a while before interrupting.

"Hey," he said softly, "are you okay?"

Simon was jolted out of his concentration.

"Oh, yeah, I'm all right. It's just that I can't get that feeling back, and I wanted so much to paint it."

"What feeling?" asked Ronald.

"Do you remember those mornings," Simon answered, "when we would sit by the spot where the water flows? Just next to that willow tree?"

"Yep," answered Ronald. "What about it?"

"And we would sit there, early in the morning just as the sun was coming up, and the sunlight kind of tickled the water and the reeds. I just can't find the words for it. It was as if the water flowed right through us. And the light, oh my, the light filled everything, too."

"Yeah," replied Ronald, "amazing moments, aren't they?"

"Right," said Simon. "But you know, when I still had all that guilt and stuff after I threw my paints into the pond, I couldn't feel the water or the light. Everything felt heavy and dark. I hated that. "

"So things got worse before they got better?" asked Ronald.

"Yeah. At night, it seemed as if the frogs were all shouting nasty things at me. I just felt worse and worse."

"So what happened?"

"Well," replied Simon, "as soon as I cleaned up the pond and the guilt left, I felt this sort of lightness and felt connected to the frogs and the pond. For the last few days, when I watch the water and the light, everything feels so close. Even more than before. It's so beautiful, all I do is start to cry!"

"Is that why you're sitting here right now?" asked Ronald.

"I'm just trying to paint that amazing feeling," said Simon. "I didn't have words to describe it, and now I don't have the colors."

"Well," said Ronald, thinking out loud, "it just may have to stay that way."

Chapter

Simon and Ronald had traveled quite a distance. For Simon, it had been a journey of discovery as well as miles. He was so far from his old shell that he found it hard even to remember it. It was as if it had never existed.

In the time he had spent with Ronald, he had seen and experienced things that had once been unimaginable. The sunrises and sunsets he could see from his new vantage point were breathtaking. Some of the creatures he'd met in the marsh were exciting and some frightening: the beavers building their homes of sticks and branches, the wise owl observing everything below, the tiny fish that populated the waters, the curious fox that lurked at the edge of the marsh, the rabbits and birds constantly searching for things to nibble on, and, of course, his new, dear friends, the bullfrogs and their families.

The tall grasses, tiny flowers, and occasional tree were part of his world as never before. And the water never looked so beautiful, so graceful, and so necessary. It was as if the water kept everything going and brought life from one end of the marsh to the other. Simon was one happy turtle.

Things weren't always perfect, however. Being out of his shell, especially around that fox, still made him nervous, and rightly so. Lightning, thunder, and heavy rains felt much different without his shell. There were days when he worried about his next meal, and when Ronald was off on one of his projects, he simply felt alone.

He had learned to use his radar to find his way through the days and nights in the marsh. Actually, he was developing a bit of a swagger, not unlike the one that Ronald sported. He couldn't predict his future, but felt up to whatever it might bring.

Now the two friends were sitting on a fallen log, warmed by the sun.

"Why can't it always be this good?" Simon asked of his tiny friend.

"It can, a lot of the time," replied Ronald. "But things change, and change isn't always easy, you know. Remember how hard it was to leave your shell?"

"Yeah. I hated that," said Simon.

"But you had to do it, didn't you?" asked Ronald.

"Yep."

"And looking back on it all, would you do it again?"

"Yep, again."

"If it was always this way, we might get bored. We might get stuck. If I hadn't changed, and if you hadn't, we never would have met each other. We wouldn't be sitting on this log together."

"But how have you changed? You always seem to have all the answers," said Simon.

"I didn't always live in this marsh," Ronald answered. "Remember, I started out in an alley. Rough times there."

"And...?"

"And I had to learn a lot really fast. That's why that old man was so important."

Moments passed. To Simon, It felt as if something were shifting.

"So, will we always be together like this? You know, friends on a log?" Simon asked.

Ronald paused. His face clouded a bit.

"Not always, but a lot of the time, especially at times like birthdays, or your coming-out-of-the-shell anniversary. And times when you" he paused, "or... I, just need to talk." Ronald grinned. "I feel excited when I think of a reunion, or a birthday, or that anniversary. They're sort of like the marsh water, coming and going."

Simon was quiet for some time. At last, he let out a sigh.

"Yeah, I guess that's how it is," he said. "Just like water."

"You've learned to travel on your own. You've got your own radar working now, and don't always need mine to get you through," said Ronald. "So I'll come and go, but you'll always have what it takes to find your way."

Along with the sadness of the going of things, the excitement of his dream returned to Simon. He saw himself moving through the marshlands, taking care of himself, listening to his radar, making decisions.

"I wonder if I'll come across some marsh critters that need to hear some of the things I've learned from you."

"Wouldn't surprise me," said Ronald. "Just pass it on. And maybe some day you'll have children, a family... Hey, you could teach them."

This new picture took Simon's breath away. It was beyond anything he had ever dreamed. An entire family of turtles, a life outside the shell with the radar to make it happen... and a new marshland where turtles, frogs, squirrels and foxes understood each other.

"Oh, my!" he exclaimed. "The marsh would just be an unbelievable place then, wouldn't it?"

As they sat, it was as if a mantle were being passed from mouse to turtle. Both were deeply grateful, and both seemed to know that hope would endure.

The User's Guide...

For parents, teachers and therapists

By Andrew Seubert, LPC, NCC
with scenario contributions from
David Mandelbaum, Ph.D.

Ronald Says...

The following is a summary of what Ronald describes as, "the four steps to becoming an emotional expert." It is quoted from a letter Ronald sent to Simon during one of his goodwill trips to the far side of the marsh.

Summer, 2014

My dear friend Simon,

Before I left on this trip I had a lot on my mind, so I didn't have time to answer your question. I had to decide if I was going to help my cousins rebuild their home after the most recent flood damaged it, or if I should try to convince them to move elsewhere. I thought they might prefer our part of the marsh where things seem safer. On the way, I stopped by Habitat for Critters. They convinced me to help them rebuild, so I took their advice. After all, they sent some of their best builders (a few robins, a beaver and a ground hog) to help us out.

Before I left, you asked me if I could put everything I taught you about your radar into a few easy-to-learn steps so that you could pass them on to your children. At first I thought, "That's crazy! You can't put all this stuff into steps!" It's kind of a flow, y'know? Like the water.

But the more I thought about it, I realized you had asked a great question. And great questions lead to great information. So here it goes, as in **A-B-C-D**!

A Be **Aware** of the feeling.
You've gotta notice that it's there. Also, make sure you check out the body for signs of the feeling. It's where the radar first shows up.

B **Be** with the feeling.
You've gotta spend time with the feeling. Pay attention to it. But make sure that you're in charge of the feeling by breathing into it and letting it go. Remember, you should have the feeling instead of allowing the feeling to have you! When you're paying attention to the feeling and managing it, then you can go onto the next step.

C **Check** the message of the feeling.
Now that you're paying attention and have calmed the feeling down a bit, you can check out the message it's bringing you. Remember, the feeling is a radar signal asking you to check out the message. It's only the messenger, not the judge and jury.

D **Decide** to express, act (or not).
This step is optional. You don't really have to do anything once you've checked out the message. But remember, if the feeling keeps on bothering you, it may be trying to get you going. Sometimes we just need to say or do something for the feeling to move on.

So that's it for now, my friend. We'll talk more after I get back. In the meantime, watch over our corner of the marsh for me, and paint your heart out. It's a great heart!

Fondly,
Your friend, Ronald

Simon Says...

Simon thinks of passing on what he has learned to his own children some day. But thoughts and questions stream through his brain, just like the marsh waters. The following are some of his questions and suggestions for each chapter to help you become an expert about your own emotional radar.

For parents, teachers and therapists:

Please use these questions as a springboard. Change them, add to them, do whatever would make them as relevant as possible for the young ones – either individually or in group - entrusted to your care. Page references after "Questions for the Reader" are from The Courage to Feel, where exercises can be found to enhance various emotional skills.

Questions from Simon

- What are the feelings that I mostly lived with inside my shell?
- Where in my body did I feel them?
- What did the feelings do for me?

Practice Scenario for Chapter 1

Claire, a 12-year old girl, has always struggled with the idea of sleepovers and, in fact, has never been on one. She has just changed schools and is invited to a sleep-over by one of the more popular girls in the class and she really wants to go. After accepting the invitation, she changes her mind the night of the event and decides to stay home.

Scenario Questions:

1. What do you think Claire was feeling when asked to the sleepover?
2. As the night approached what do you think happened for Claire regarding her change of heart? What might she have been saying to herself about going to the sleep-over?
3. What kinds of feelings might Claire have been experiencing when she was at home and knowing that other girls were at the party?
4. What skill enables Claire to notice all of these things?

Questions for the Reader (Courage to Feel, Ch. 1, 2 and 3)

- How do you learn to notice feelings?
- Where do you feel them?
- What do they do for you?
- What are different feelings trying to tell you?

Questions from Simon

- **How did I learn to be afraid?**
- **What other feeling came into the picture?**
- **Where in my body did I feel these new feelings?**

Practice Scenario for Chapters 2-3

You are 15 years old and you've agreed to dog sit and dog walk for a neighbor who was to be out of town for the weekend. The neighbor lives within a couple of blocks and your neighborhood is pretty safe, a typical suburb. On Friday, early evening, you leave the house to do your job. It's still light and the sun is just going down. As you leave, your mother calls you back and insists on driving you to the neighbor's. You insist that it's safe enough for you to walk, but your mom persists and she drives you to the neighbor's home.

Scenario Questions:

1. What feelings do you experience when this happens?
2. Where did you notice them in your body?
3. What is an assumption?
4. What are you assuming your mom thinks/believes about you?
5. What do you think some of your mom's feelings might be?
6. Can you think of a time (or times) when you thought your mother or father was being overprotective?
7. How did you feel about what they did?
8. What were your feelings telling you about mom's decision?

Questions for the Reader (Courage to Feel, Ch. 7)

- What kinds of things are you afraid of?
- How did you learn that?
- What are some of the messages in your family about feelings?
- Are the messages spoken or unspoken?
- Does your family appreciate the cautious approach of Simon's mother or the more adventurous approach of Ronald the mouse?
- Perhaps it is something in the middle or completely different?

Questions from Simon

- What was the lion in my dream trying to tell me?
- Which feelings were upsetting me?
- Does that mean the feelings are "bad"?
- Was I afraid or excited or both?

Questions for the Reader (Courage to Feel, Ch. 7 and 8)

- **Do you ever have dreams that leave you with feelings?**
- **Which feelings upset you?**
- **Do you think some feelings are bad? Which ones?**
- **Have you ever felt more than one feeling at a time?**
- **How does it feel when you agree with your family's message about feelings?**
- **How does it feel when you disagree with their message about feelings?**

Questions from Simon

- What was I dreaming more and more about doing?
- What feelings took place in my dreams?
- Where in my body did I feel them?
- Is my relationship with my mother unhealthy?
- What did I do differently for the first time ever?
- What does Ronald mean by “head and heart”?
- What might I have been hopeful about?
- Even if I was still afraid, was it still okay to feel hopeful?
- What did my mom teach me about other turtles?

Practice Scenario for Chapter 4-6

Jason is a 12 year-old boy and, since the age of 5, has been a soccer player. His parents signed him up for a traveling team, and he has played both for his schools and a local league. His parents have taken great pride and joy in his skills and success. A conflict arose for Jason during the past year, in that he has developed a strong interest and shown a great deal of potential in art. He doesn't want to do the traveling team and would rather spend that time taking art lessons and joining an art club after school.

Scenario Questions:

1. How would you describe the conflict that Jason is feeling?
2. What might be some of his feelings and what are the messages that go with those feelings?
3. What is he imagining that his parents would think if he told them of his new interest and desire? What is he most afraid of?
4. What might he be thinking about himself because of his new interest?
5. What might he start to feel if he didn't follow his interest in art?

Questions for the Reader (Courage to Feel, Ch. 5)

- What kinds of things do you dream about most?
- What feelings do you notice in your dreams?
- Where in your body do you feel them?
- Do fear and hope and excitement feel different?
- What does "dysfunctional" mean?
- Have you ever felt dysfunctional? What was it like?
- Have you ever tried to do something new?
- Did your thoughts and feelings collide?
- What are you hopeful about?
- Have you ever been afraid to follow your dreams?
- Is it easier for you to be like other kids or different?
- How can you manage difficult feelings?

Questions from Simon

- What did I have to learn to do in order to relax enough to get out of my shell?
- What was the magic word?
- What did it mean for me to leave home?
- What would my mom do if she caught me outside my shell?
- What feeling was I afraid of the most?

Questions for the Reader (Courage to Feel, Ch. 17 and 18)

- What do you do to relax?
- Do you have a magic word to help you relax?
- Ronald tells Simon he is making his mother's world his own; what does this mean?
- What was Ronald's advice?
- What changes have you made so far in your life?
- If so, what feelings came up when you were doing that?
- What changes would you like to make in the future?
- What feelings come up when you think of or make those changes?
- Are they mixed feelings?
- What feelings are you most afraid of?

Questions from Simon

- What feelings was my mother experiencing?
- How did I know she was experiencing those feelings?
- What are my mother's two greatest fears?
- What, according to Ronald, would happen if I got hurt?
- What did Ronald remind me to do so that I could calm down and tell my mom the truth?
- What was the "something larger" that I experienced with Ronald and my mother?
- What other feelings were present?

Questions for the Reader (Courage to Feel, Ch. 4)

- What feelings do others around you have?
- How can you tell someone else's feelings?
- Do you know when someone else is afraid?
- What can you do if you get hurt?
- Have you ever been so nervous that you couldn't calm your feelings down?
- What would help?

Questions from Simon

- What was the "bad" feeling I experienced?
- What was it about my mom that set that feeling off?
- What was Ronald was trying to get me to do with all his questions?
- What was the next thing that I had to do to clear up my confusion?
- What was the deeper feeling that looked like anger on my mom's face?
- Once my mom and I were clear about our feelings, what changed?
- How did we clear things up?

Practice Scenario for Chapter 7

Susan, age 17, has consistently been encouraged by her parents to take the most challenging honors and advanced placement classes, so that she might earn a scholarship to college, something which would help the family finances enormously. The problem is that Susan feels overwhelmed and believes that she isn't having a "normal" high school experience, because she doesn't have the time to do extracurriculars and have typical social experiences. She decides to take only honors classes and eliminate the advanced placements. She tells her mother, and her mom, while expressing some concern, agrees to Susan's decision. A week later Susan perceives her mother as being upset when Susan tells her of an upcoming date..

Scenario Questions:

1. Story telling is when we assume something is true without clear evidence to support the story. What story might Susan be making up about her mother's apparent reaction to her date?
2. How might she be feeling as a result of the story she is telling herself?
3. What can she do to get more factual information to either prove or disprove the story about her mom's reaction?

Questions for the Reader (Courage to Feel, Ch. 11)

- What are some bad feelings you have experienced?
- What or who sets your feelings off?
- What kinds of stories do you tell yourself when you are set off?
- What if this trigger is a false alarm?
- In whom have you confided your stories?
- How does their perception of your story differ from how you feel?
- What can you do to help others understand your own feelings and story?

Questions from Simon

- What were some of the feelings I was having when Ronald came by to where I was painting?
- What colors was I using?
- What did Ronald suggest I do?
- What was the feeling underneath the first ones?

Practice Scenario for Chapter 8

Michael is a 17 year-old boy who is extremely close to his grandfather. His pop-pop has been a mentor to him all his young life, teaching him how to hunt, fish and repair just about anything that needed to be fixed. He's been noticing that his grandfather's thinking and memory seem to be going downhill and doesn't seem to be able to care for himself as well as he always could. Michael was doing a repair job for his mother when he started crying in the middle of it.

Scenario Questions:

1. **Why do you think Michael started to cry as he was repairing his mom's refrigerator?**
2. **Besides sadness at the deterioration of his grandfather, what other feelings might he be experiencing?**
3. **As much as he loves his grandfather, Michael sometimes experiences anger towards him as well. How would you understand that anger if you were in Michael's place? Could the anger be sitting on top of another feeling? If so, what feeling?**

Questions for the Reader (Courage to Feel, Ch. 8)

- **Is there a word to describe how sometimes one feeling sits underneath another one?**
- **Have you ever had that happen to you?**

Questions from Simon

- **What did Ronald suggest I do when I had all kinds of feelings and I didn't know what to do about them?**
- **What's this "voice" that Ronald is talking about?**
- **What did Ronald do to avoid listening to his inner voice?**
- **What happened to Ronald when he listened to his inner voice?**

Practice Scenario for Chapter 9

Robert, age 13, is about to leave for a four-week summer camp in about a month. He has always wanted to go and has been very excited about attending. However, he is already starting to feel nervous and homesick, although his departure is a month away. He's begun to think how miserable he'd be away from home, even though he thinks his parents are jerks, anyway. Quite a problem!

Scenario Questions:

1. What stories do you think Robert is making up about himself and his time away?
2. Do you think not going would be the best decision? Why or why not?
3. Which feelings should he listen to?
4. What might Robert do to help himself make the best decision possible?

Questions for the Reader (Courage to Feel, Ch. 9)

- What should you do when you have feelings you can't understand?
- Do you have an inner voice?
- What do you do to avoid listening to yours?
- Can you trust your inner voice?
- Have you ever listened to it? And what happened?
- What happens when you don't listen to that inner voice?
- Give an example or two.

Questions from Simon

- Why was it so important for me to want things to stay the same all the time?
- Did feelings tell me how things were outside?
- Could I count on my feelings to tell me the truth?
- Are my feelings a type of "radar"?
- What colored the way I saw things?
- How did leaving my shell change me?

Practice Scenario for Chapter 10

Carl is a high school senior, captain of the school's basketball team. The day before, the team lost a close game to a traditional rival, a game they should have won. The following morning he awoke with a headache and a queasy stomach. The last thing he wanted to do was to go to school and have to interact with his schoolmates. As he sat down at the breakfast table, everything his mother and his younger brother said or did annoyed him. His father called him on his behavior: "What's the matter with you?" "Nothin'!!" was Carl's reply. And this mood continued throughout the day at school.

Scenario Questions:

1. What really was the matter with Carl?
2. Was his problem physical, emotional, both?
3. What kind of feelings could he have been experiencing before going to bed? And upon awakening the next morning?
4. How does he see his family through the lens of these feelings? Who has changed – Carl's family or Carl?
5. How does he see his schoolmates?
6. What might Carl do to change the way he experiences everyone on this day?

Questions for the Reader (Courage to Feel, Ch. 11)

- What feelings come up for you when things change?
- Do feelings tell you how things are outside? Inside? Or both?
- Is it the job of feelings to tell you exactly how things are?
- What's the job of radar? Of feelings?
- What colors the way you see things or the way you perceive things?
- How has any decision to change made you different?

Questions from Simon

- Was it possible for the other critters to know what I was trying to do?
- Why couldn't they figure out what I was feeling?
- What was the task that lay ahead for me after Ronald and I spoke to each other?
- Ronald had this equation: A = R = T = VR (Awareness plus Responsibility plus Telling the truth equals vital relationships). How would the equation work with the frogs?

Practice Scenario for Chapter 11

Fran, age 14, is really angry at her best friend, Sara. She believes that Sara has been ignoring her by not responding immediately to texts and not returning e-mails quickly enough.

Scenario Questions:

1. While Fran is aware of her anger, what feelings might she be experiencing that feed that feeling. In other words, might there be other feelings layered underneath her anger?
2. What stories could Fran be making up about both Sara and herself in this situation?
3. How can she check out the validity or truth to her stories?

Questions for the Reader (Courage to Feel, Ch. 12)

- Do you keep your feelings to yourself?
- Are you afraid to be open about your feelings? If so, why?
- Do you have an example when telling the truth made you feel better?
- Worse?
- Use Ronald's equation [A + R + T = VR] to brainstorm how you might clear the air with someone.

Questions from Simon

- What was I feeling so good about?
- How was I feeling about myself at that moment?
- What kinds of things did Ronald bring up that caused me not to feel so good about myself?
- Why might that be a problem for me?
- Why did I compare all of this to cloudy and sunny days?
- Is it possible to feel connected to my mom and Ronald and still feel good about myself, even when they're grumpy or irritating?

Practice Scenario for Chapter 12

Liam, a 16 year-old high school junior, is a kind and very sensitive boy. He appears to be well liked by practically everyone. Whenever someone he cares about seems upset or blue, Liam takes it upon himself to try and cheer them up. He feels responsible for everyone if they're having a bad day and tries to drop everything if a friend is in need in order to be there for them.

Scenario Questions:

1. At times, Liam feels strangely depressed when he is trying to help his friend(s). Why might that be?
2. How do you think Liam's friends might be feeling about Liam?
3. Does how a friend or family member feel ever determine how you feel? When is that good? When not?

Questions for the Reader (Courage to Feel, Ch. 13)

- **How can your feelings be separate from your surroundings?**
- **If your surroundings are sad, how do you keep yourself from being sad?**
- **What's the difference between living from the outside in and the inside out?**
- **What does it mean to be true to yourself or to hold onto yourself?**
- **What is the difference between being "lost" in someone else or "depending" on their "approval" and being "connected" to them?**

Questions from Simon

- What was I feeling sad and excited about?
- Why was that confusing?
- What was the other example Ronald used to show me how sad and glad can be there at the same time?
- And why did I get those feelings in the evening?

Practice Scenario for Chapter 13

Victoria, a 17 year-old high school graduate, was preparing to leave for college the last week in August after she graduated. She was quite thrilled to be going and had an extremely successful first semester. However, she sorely missed the closeness and the affection that she had always enjoyed with her family. When she returned home for winter break and received huge hugs from both of her parents, she burst into tears. "Why am I crying?" she blurted out. "Especially when it feels so good to be hugged again?" Days later, looking forward to her return to college, she became very sad and a little anxious, leaving her feeling confused and puzzled about all of these conflicting emotions.

Scenario Questions:

1. Why would hugs from her parents bring Victoria to tears?
2. What did being home represent for Victoria?
3. What did going back to school bring up for her?
4. Can you recall times when you might have felt two contradictory feelings at the same time and how did you eventually come to understand it?

Questions for the Reader (Courage to Feel, Ch. 14)

- What makes you glad or excited?
- What about sad or excited feelings confuses you?
- Have you ever felt glad and sad at the same time?
- Do certain feelings come at the same time?

Questions from Simon

- How did the marsh feel on this particular day?
- What kind of feeling did it bring up or trigger in Ronald?
- What were Ronald's parents like?
- In telling his story about the alley up north, what did Ronald share about things he had learned from his old friend?
- What was the last present the old man gave Ronald before he lost his sight?
- What did Ronald offer me as an explanation as to how we can feel warm and sad at the same time?
- What did I become sad about?
- How is this possible? And what's an emotional *trigger*?
- What present experiences trigger or connect to past memories for Ronald?

Practice Scenario for Chapter 14

Carl is a very driven kind of kid. He always has to do things perfectly, be the best or, at least, be among the best. Both of his parents are career people, A-type personalities, who have always been demanding of their children, especially of Carl, their oldest, rarely complimenting him for all his efforts. As soon as he turned 16, Carl applied for and got a job at a local McDonalds. Not long after he began his new job, he started to feel uncomfortable when his supervisor praised him, telling him that his best was always good enough. The supervisor expressed great appreciation of Carl and took Carl under his wing. "Kids like you," the supervisor said to Carl one day, "are a gift! Thank you." With those words, tears began to stream down Carl's face.

Scenario Questions:

1. Why would such a compliment bring tears to Carl's eyes?
2. What mixture of feelings is Carl experiencing?
3. What's the connection between his home life and his job?
4. What's the emotional trigger for Carl?

Questions for the Reader (Courage to Feel, Ch. 13)

- What feeling do you have on a cloudy day?
- Is it hard for you when those close to you are experiencing difficult feelings? What can you do then?
- Is there anyone you know with whom you can share stories and feelings?
- What makes that possible?
- Has anyone else's sadness ever awakened your own sadness?
- Give an example of a present experience that reminds you of a positive past experience and that triggers a mixture of feelings.

Questions from Simon

- **What was the strange sight that Ronald came across at the start of this chapter?**
- **What was I trying to do?**
- **What had I done that was so bad?**
- **What was I hiding from and was hiding helping?**
- **What feeling(s) do you think I was experiencing after doing something like that?**
- **Wasn't I bad or isn't there something wrong with me for doing such a thing?**

Practice Scenario for Chapter 15

David, a 15 year-old counselor-in-training at a summer sleepaway camp, had a best friend, Gerry. Gerry had confided to David that when he was much younger he had an extremely unpleasant and embarrassing experience where he threw up some blood clots. Later in the summer David played what he thought was a practical joke. He piled all the red jello on a plate front of Gerry's chair. Gerry looked at David, teared up and left the table.

Scenario Questions:

1. What do you think was the main feeling Gerry had?
2. How about David?
3. What action or actions can David take to try and stay friends with Gerry?
4. If David tells himself "I blew it!", what feeling might he be experiencing? If he tells himself "I'm a total screw up", what feeling might he be experiencing then?

Questions for the Reader (Courage to Feel, Ch. 16)

- Have you ever done something wrong or “bad”?
- Did you feel like a “bad” person?
- What feelings came up for you then?
- Were you actually a bad person?
- How did you handle it then?
- How would you handle it now?

Questions from Simon

- What choices did I have after that incident?
- Is guilt a "bad" feeling?
- What's the purpose of guilt?
- What could I learn from my guilt?
- What other feeling came up when I began to believe that I was the worst turtle in the world?
- Is that different from my guilty feeling?
- Are "doing bad" and "being bad" the same?

Practice Scenario for Chapter 16

David, who had put the jello in front of Gerry in an earlier scenario, saw the look of pain on his friend's face. During the rest period right after lunch, David asked if he could talk to Gerry. Gerry was lying face down on his bunk and didn't respond. David apologized and asked for forgiveness. Gerry still didn't respond. David then walked away and lay on his bunk.

Scenario Questions:

1. **What do you think David felt?**
2. **Why do you think Gerry didn't respond?**
3. **What do you think David could or should do now going forward? Is there anything else to do other than apologize?**

Questions for the Reader (Courage to Feel, Ch. 5 and 16)

- When have you felt guilty?
- What did you do with the guilty feeling?
- Do you think that guilt is supposed to punish you?
- Are guilt and "ashamed" the same or different?
- What's the message that "ashamed" delivers?
- Have you ever felt ashamed?
- Does that feeling make you the worst person in the world?
- How would you check out the message of ashamed?
- Are you good at separating what people do from who they are?

Questions from Simon

- After I had my "tantrum," what did most of the frogs think of turtles?
- What did I do to make it better and to help the frogs understand me better?
- What did I need to learn about the frogs' singing to stop judging them and to understand them better?

Practice Scenario for Chapter 17-18

Lois, a 12 year-old seventh grader, had started a rumor about another classmate, Nancy. It was a very mean spirited rumor having to do with Nancy and a boy. It wasn't true. Nancy and her friends retaliated by spreading false rumors about Lois. These exchanges continued until it was obvious to the principal that something had to be done. She called a meeting for all seventh graders to attend a morning assembly.

Scenario Questions:

1. Why would anyone start rumors?
2. What kinds of feelings might motivate creating rumors?
3. What might be some of Lois' beliefs about herself that would lead to creating rumors?
4. How do you think Nancy felt when she first heard the rumor?
5. Do you believe she was justified in retaliating the way she did?
6. Did Lois and Nancy really understand or get each other? How do you think their friends started to react?
7. What other options were open to Nancy in her response?
8. If you were the principal, what would you say to the students?

Questions for the Reader (Courage to Feel, Ch. 7 and 12)

- **What's an assumption?**
- **Do you ever make assumptions or judgments about others?**
- **What is it like when someone makes an assumption about you?**
- **What needs to happen to keep from hurting each other through assumptions?**

Questions from Simon

- **What was the frogs' opinion of me before I spoke with them?**
- **What did we need to learn or get about each other? If things had gotten worse, what might the swamp have turned into?**

Questions for the Reader (Courage to Feel, Ch. 12 and 19)

- How do you think others perceive you?
- What happens when we don't understand what it's like for another person?
- What kind of thoughts and assumptions do we entertain when we don't really know the other person? Think of a specific person.
- Has anyone not understood and, therefore misunderstood you? A parent, friend or teacher?
- What do you think this has to do with fights between groups of people, even countries?

Questions from Simon

- What feeling did my dream leave me with?
- Did doubting my decision to leave my shell mean I had made a bad choice?
- If not, then why was I having all of those feelings that seemed to say, "Danger!"?
- What was Ronald trying to get me to do by painting the two pictures?
- How is this like watching a river?
- What did I need to learn to do with the fear?

Practice Scenario for Chapter 19

John is a 19 year-old college freshman at a music school. He is an extraordinary musician, playing many different instruments and especially gifted with the guitar, which he taught himself. He is also a brilliant young man. He was extremely depressed about being in school and dropped out after his first semester, much to the disappointment of his mother. While at home he went to therapy and realized that he wanted to play music, not learn about it. His therapist always used to say, "Listen to that quiet voice inside!" This kind of scared him, but he decided to take the risk. He picked up a part-time job in order to pay for additional music lessons, and.... the result? He is about to go on a nationwide tour with this band, no longer feels depressed and thinks about eventually going back to school. He has been supporting himself by teaching at his local School of Rock.

Scenario Questions:

1. Why do you think John felt so depressed while at school?
2. What kinds of internal and external pressures do you think John experienced both when he was in school and when he decided to risk a life of music? What kind of feelings?
3. Why did John's depression lift when he started teaching and performing?
4. Have you seen the movie "Once" [someone may have to summarize the plot]? What does the lead character teach us about listening to what we want?
5. What would be the difference between John being taken over by his depression and fears as opposed to observing them, noticing them, questioning them and learning from them?

Questions for the Reader (Courage to Feel, Ch. 3, 4, 5, and 6)

- **What kinds of self-doubt do you have?**
- **How do you distinguish between real danger and a "false alarm" fear?**
- **What's the name of the skill that lets us step back from a feeling and observe it in order to check its message?**
- **What are the steps in checking out your fear?**
- **Think of the last time that you felt sad or angry or afraid. Can you remember the situation and the details?**
- **Just watch the feeling, especially where you notice it in your body. What happens to the feeling if you watch it,**
- **let it pass through and then question its message?**

Questions from Simon

- What got worse for me before they got better?
- How did I feel before and then after I cleaned up the pond?
- When I couldn't name or paint my feeling, did that mean that I shouldn't pay attention to it? What did Ronald suggest?

Practice Scenario for Chapter 20

Back to David and Gerry again. As you might recall, David was the teen who played the jello trick on his good friend, Gerry. When we left them last, David had apologized to Gerry, but had received no response from him. Recently, Gerry started talking to David, forgave him, and they started reestablishing their relationship, eventually becoming best friends again. Even though he felt confident that the friendship was growing again, David, at times, hesitated to reach out. He felt obvious joy when thinking about his friend but, strangely, also experienced overwhelming emotion that sometimes led to tears.

Scenario Questions:

1. While David's happy feelings might be more understandable, can you think of reasons he might have experienced feelings that led to tears (hint: other than regret for past actions)?
2. What do you think David and Gerry learned from this experience about emotions and the challenges of maintaining a close friendship?
3. Have you ever felt so good about something that you simply couldn't put the feelings into words?
4. Did any of these exceptional feelings come after something bad had happened? Or after you experienced something or someone you had missed for a long time?

Questions for the Reader (Courage to Feel, Ch. 6 and 17)

- **Have you ever felt guilty, did something about it, and then felt better afterwards?**
- **What have you done to correct a wrong?**
- **What happens when you don't pay attention to your feelings, especially guilt?**
- **How do you get along with other people if you have a stockpile of feelings like guilt and anger inside?**
- **Have you ever had feeling that you couldn't put into words?**
- **Would you be willing to describe one of those moments?**

Questions from Simon

- When I was sitting on the log with Ronald, enjoying his company and our friendship, how could I feel happy and sad at the same time?
- Was I willing for things to change?
- What are the special times that Ronald mentioned when we would be together?
- I learned that our friendship was like the marsh waters. What did that mean?
- What was the vision of my future that came to me towards the end of my conversation with Ronald?
- How will my emotional radar help me live this vision?

Practice Scenario for Chapter 21

Jen is 18 and about to depart for college. She has had a very close circle of friends throughout high school, and they are all going to different colleges. At their goodbye party, there are tears and much laughter. Alice proclaims to the group that she intends to remain best friends with them all forever and awaits a similar declaration from the rest of the girls. They all immediately swear to remain best friends forever. Jen feels deeply connected to Alice and truly wants to remain friends with her forever. However, Jen is surprised by an uncomfortable sensation in her stomach after she confirms her intention to remain friends with Alice.

Scenario Questions:

1. Given what you've been learning about emotions, what might Jen be thinking to cause her that uncomfortable sensation?
2. Can you think of times in your life when close friends seem to have drifted away from you and what your beliefs were about that?
3. How do close relationships change or even fade away over time and what do you think about the relationships after they've changed or faded?
4. Are you comfortable with things changing?
5. What feelings do you sometimes experience when friendships change or even end? What can you do with those feelings?
6. Can thoughts or memories help you remain connected to others even when you know that the relationship might end some day?

Questions for the Reader (Courage to Feel, Ch. 13 and 17)

- Have you ever had the experience of feeling happy and sad at the same time?
- How would you explain that?
- Do you like change? Yes? No?
- What are special times for you and your friends to be together?
- Do friendships always stay the same?
- What feelings might you experience if they do change?
- What kind of vision do you have for your life?
- How about for just this year? Next year? When you're older?
- How will your feelings help you do all this?
- And the biggest question of all, what shell do you need to leave behind?

Finally, my friends, whatever your vision and your dreams might be, remember to use your magnificent emotional radar. It has simply changed my entire life. Be well, be good to yourself and make your marsh a better place in which to live.

Bye for now,
Simon.

Contributors

David Mandelbaum, Ph.D.

David is a psychologist in private practice in Wilmington, DE, with over 30 years specializing in working with adolescents and their families. He is the author of several book chapters on the subject of therapy with young people.

Email contact: DMPHD@aol.com

Marc Rubin

Marc paints still lifes that invite meaning and evoke story. He captures everyday objects at eye-level and sized in the frame as they are in the world—but he imbues them with a spirit and presence so that, emotionally, they become larger than life. Rubin's masterfully painted representational oils are exhibited in galleries throughout the Northeast. In addition to his work as a painter, Marc is an award-winning graphic designer and owner of Marc Rubin Associates, Elmira, NY. Be sure to check out Marc's doodles!

Visit Marc at http://www.marcrubinassociates.com

Contributors

Andrew Seubert, LPC, NCC

Andrew is the co-founder of ClearPath Healing Arts Center in Corning, NY and Seneca Lake, NY. A licensed psychotherapist for 30 years, he has an extensive background in Existential-Gestalt psychotherapy and provides EMDR consultation and training for other clinicians. Andrew specializes in working with trauma, PTSD, eating disorders and the integration of spirituality and psychotherapy. A passionate and engaging international presenter and workshop facilitator, Andrew lives with his wife, Barbara and their dog Nellie, canine resplendent, on Seneca Lake, NY. Andrew and Barbara have co-parented a blended family of five. Visit Andrew and Barbara at http://www.clearpathhealingarts.com.

Caitlin Turner

Caitlin received her BFA from the Rhode Island School of Design in 2011. She currently works as a freelance illustrator in upstate New York and has plans on pursuing a degree in graphic design. To see her work you can visit her website at http://www.caitlineturner.com.

CPSIA information can be obtained at www.ICGtesting.com
Printed in the USA
BVOW04s1033130815

413086BV00004B/8/P